BAZ & BENZ

HEiDi McKinnon

SIMON & SCHUSTER BOOKS FOR YOUNG READERS
An imprint of Simon & Schuster Children's Publishing Division
1230 Avenue of the Americas, New York, New York 10020

Benz, are we friends?

Yes, Baz, we are bestest friends.

For how long?

Forever and ever.

What if I turned purple?

That would be funny!
But I would still be your friend.

What if I turned purple
and had spots?

That would be REALLY funny!

What if I said MEEP
all the time?

That would be annoying.

Meep!

Meep! Meep!

mmeeeEEP!

MEEP! MEEP! MEEP!

MEEP!

That would be

reaLLy
annoying!

MEEP!

Stop.

What if I disappeared?

**Then I would be sad
and miss you a lot.**

But I would still be your friend . . .

Forever and ever.

Because you are you.

Meep!

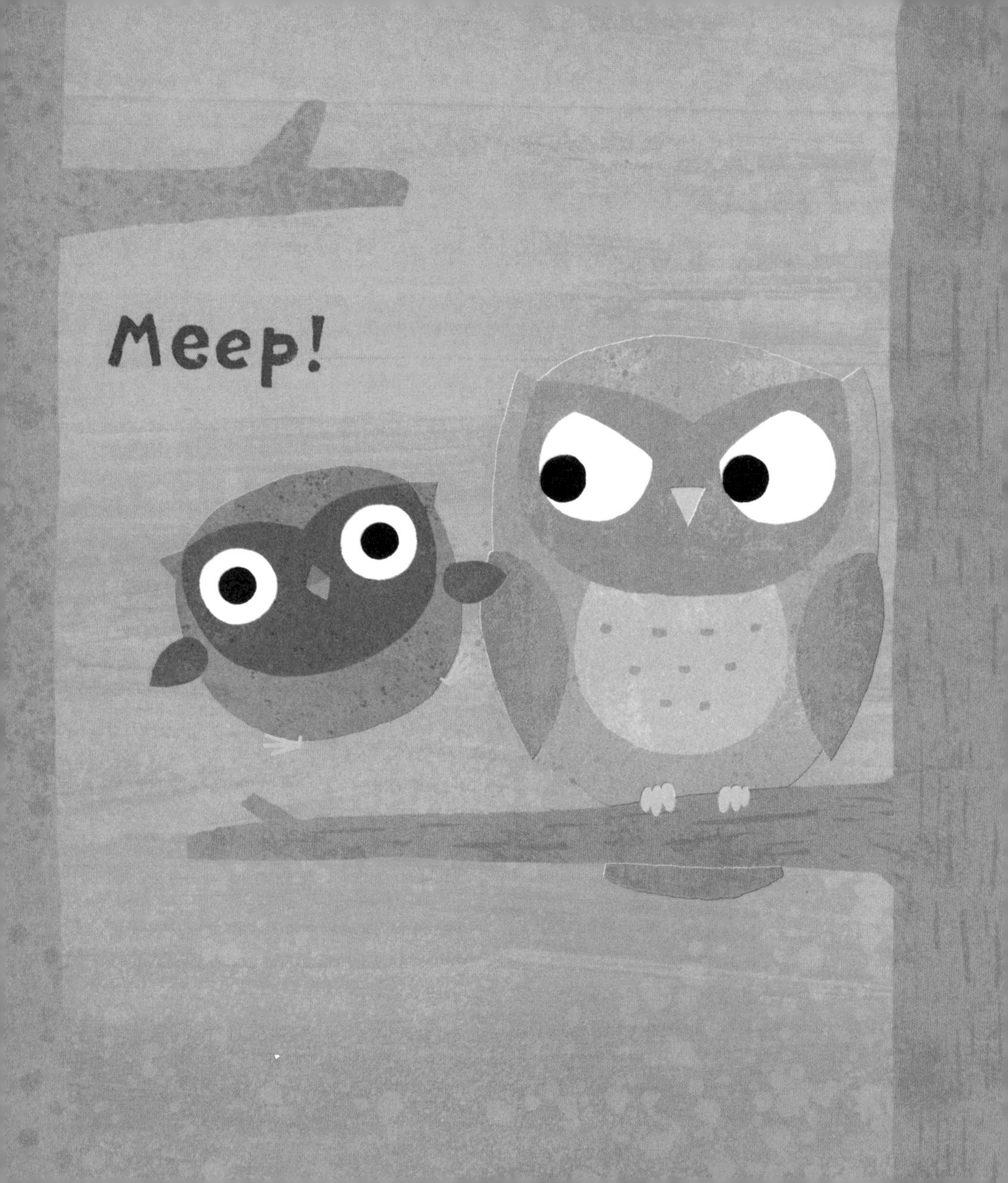